TRIPLET TROUBLE
and
the Red Heart Race

**There are more books about the
Tucker Triplets!**

Triplet Trouble and the
Talent Show Mess

Triplet Trouble and the
Runaway Reindeer

Coming soon
Triplet Trouble and the
Field Day Disaster

TRIPLET TROUBLE
and
the Red Heart Race

by Debbie Dadey and Marcia Thornton Jones
Illustrated by John Speirs

A
LITTLE APPLE
PAPERBACK

SCHOLASTIC INC.
New York Toronto London Auckland Sydney

ISBN 0-590-58106-6

12 11 10   3 4 5 6 7 8 9/0

Printed in the U.S.A.   40

First Scholastic Printing, January 1996

Contents

1. St. Valentine's Day   1
2. Truckload   6
3. Heart Heaven   12
4. The Red Heart Race   19
5. Seeing Red   27
6. The Red Heart Mess   33
7. Ashley's Brilliant Idea   39
8. A Secret   44

1

St. Valentines Day

"Good morning, class," Mr. Parker said with a big smile. "We have a special project this morning."

Everyone groaned except for Adam Tucker. Adam is the smartest kid in second grade. He leaned closer to read the sign Mr. Parker was holding. Mr. Parker's

signs usually mean more work. It said
VALENTINE CARDS.

I groaned again, but Ashley Tucker
giggled. Ashley is Adam's sister and she
giggles a lot. "I think valentines are SO
cute!" Ashley said. "And St. Valentine's
Day is only two days away."

Making valentines isn't my favorite
thing to do. I bet it isn't Adam's either.
My name is Sam Johnson and I'd rather
draw pictures of airplanes. I looked over
at Alex Tucker. Everyone else in the class
was drawing hearts on pieces of red paper.
Everyone but Alex and me.

Alex is Adam's and Ashley's sister.
They are triplets. I like them all, but Alex
and I are best friends. "What's wrong?" I
whispered to Alex.

2

"Valentines are dumb," Alex said, sticking out her lip.

Ashley turned around and looked at her sister. "You just say that because you can't make even one itty bitty valentine that's pretty."

"I can too!" Alex said.

"Cannot," Ashley said.

Alex stared at Ashley. I stared at both of them. I didn't like the way they were looking at each other. When Alex and Ashley get mad there is usually trouble.

I looked down at my red paper. I decided to get busy on my valentines and forget about Alex and Ashley. Then I had an idea. I would make valentines with airplanes on them. Maybe if I told Alex about my idea she'd make airplane valentines, too. I started to tell her, but I was too late.

Alex was having her own brilliant idea. I can always tell when she is coming up with a plan. Her eyes get big and round. Then she snaps her fingers right in front of her nose. I know exactly what that means. It means trouble.

2

Truckload

"I can make more valentines than anybody in this room," Alex said.

Ashley stuck her nose in the air. "Go ahead, see if I care." Ashley turned around and started cutting her red paper.

Alex drew and drew. Then she cut and cut. A big stack of red valentines grew on the corner of her desk. She went to the art table and got a big handful of red paper. Mr. Parker looked up from the papers he was grading and rubbed his chin, but he didn't say anything.

Alex sat back down. She drew and cut. I was still working on my first valentine. I made a blue jet airplane with green wheels. I wrote in orange letters:

Roses are red,
Jets go high,
Be My Valentine or
Away I'll Fly.

I can't fly, of course, but it did rhyme. Maybe I could give it to my dad. He would probably think it was funny. He likes planes, too.

I looked over at Alex. Her desk looked like a truckload of valentines was dumped on it. There were even red valentines scattered all over the floor around her desk.

"All right," Mr. Parker said after clearing his throat. "It's clean-up time."

Alex scrambled on the floor to pick up the dropped valentines. "I made more valentines than you," Alex whispered to Ashley.

"Want to bet?" Ashley said. She pointed to her desk. She had three huge stacks of hearts. One stack was red, one was white, and one was pink. Each stack was very neat.

Not only did Ashley have a ton of valentines, but so did Maria and Barbara who sat next to her. I had never seen so many valentines in my life.

Valentines are supposed to make you feel better, at least that's what I thought. But for some reason, seeing all those big stacks of red, white, and pink didn't make me feel better. It made me worried. Very worried.

3

Heart Heaven

Adam shook his head and looked at Alex. "You look like you died and went to heart heaven."

Ashley giggled and I nodded. It was after school and we were walking home.

Alex had spent every spare moment at school decorating herself with hearts. Now she had hearts taped to her coat. She

had hearts stuck in her hair. She even had hearts on her shoelaces. Alex always tried to be different than her brother and sister. Today she looked very different.

"Mr. Parker is going to get mad if you use all of his red paper," I told Alex.

"No, he won't," Alex said. "He told us to make valentines so we'll be ready for our Valentine's Day party."

Ashley looked at her sister. "But he didn't tell us to make a million of them."

"You made a bunch, too," Alex said.

Ashley shrugged. "I can't help it if I love valentines!"

"I've decided that I like them, too," Alex said.

We stopped walking and stood in front of the Oakridge Retirement Home. I

looked at my watch. It was exactly 3:15. Miss Crankshaw looked out of her window and waved. We waved back.

Alex sighed as we started walking again. "It's too bad Miss Crankshaw had to move there," she said. "I liked it better when she lived on our street."

"You just liked the cookies she baked," Adam said.

Alex smiled, showing the big space where her front tooth was missing.

I liked Miss Crankshaw. She made yummy cookies before she fell and hurt her hip. She also told us great stories about life in the old days. She had known Charles Lindbergh, the first pilot to fly across the Atlantic Ocean all by himself.

"Maybe we could make her some cookies," I said.

"That's a great idea," Alex said. "Let's do it right now!"

Ashley shook her head. "I can't. I'm going over to Barbara's house to make more valentines."

"We should do our homework first," Adam said.

Ashley and Adam went into their house.

Alex followed me to my house. "Do you want to work on our homework together?" I asked.

"No," Alex said, patting my dog, Cleo. She pulled a handful of valentines out of her pocket and poked a hole in each of them. Then she pulled some of Cleo's hair through the holes. Pretty soon, Cleo looked like she had exploded with valentines. Cleo looked at me and whined.

"I don't think Cleo likes those hearts," I said.

"Of course she does," Alex said. "Everybody likes hearts." Then she snapped her fingers right in front of her nose. "The world would be a better place if there were more hearts," she said. "Lots more hearts!"

"More hearts?" I asked. I had the feeling that homework and making cookies were the last thing on Alex's mind right now. Whatever she was thinking, I hoped it wouldn't be too terrible.

4

The Red Heart Race

It was the day before Valentine's Day. Mr. Parker looked around the room. He stopped when he saw Alex. Everybody stared at Alex. She had red hearts pinned to her pink shirt. She had red hearts glued to her blue jeans. She even had red hearts tied to twenty tiny ponytails. Alex smiled.

Mr. Parker smiled back. He rubbed his

chin and then turned around to write math problems on the board. That's when Alex went into action. She grabbed a crayon from her school box and scribbled on the back of her homework. Then she held up her sign so the kids in Mr. Parker's second grade could see. In messy purple letters it said Red Heart Race.

Mr. Parker turned around and Alex slapped the paper flat on her desk. Ashley giggled. So did Barbara and Maria. I shook my head. If Alex wasn't careful, there was going to be trouble.

Alex bent over her paper and pretended to work. As soon as Mr. Parker turned away, Alex scribbled with her purple crayon again. When she held up her sign it said First One to Make 100 Wins!

Adam rolled his eyes. Barbara went back to working. But Ashley stared at Alex's sign until Mr. Parker turned around again.

"Alex," Mr. Parker said in his serious voice. "Why aren't you working on the math problems?"

Alex's face turned as red as the hearts tied in her hair. Then her eyes got big. I held my breath. She was thinking up another one of her brilliant ideas. Finally, she snapped her fingers right in front of her nose.

"This IS math," Alex told him. "A valentine math project!"

Mr. Parker sighed. "You'll have to work on that project later. Right now, you should be doing the problems from the board."

For the rest of the morning Alex worked. At least while Mr. Parker was looking. But whenever he turned away, Alex snipped at red paper. By lunchtime she had already made enough red hearts to cover her desk.

"You're going to get in trouble," Adam told her. "Big trouble."

Alex shook her head so hard a red heart fell from her hair and landed in Ashley's applesauce. "I'm going to win the race," Alex said loudly enough for everyone at the table to hear.

Ashley picked the soggy heart from her applesauce. "Nobody's racing you," she told her sister.

Alex grinned. "You're afraid I'll beat you."

"Am not," Ashley said.

"Me, neither," Barbara said.

"I'm the best valentine maker in the entire school," Maria bragged.

Maria stared at Barbara. Barbara stared at Ashley. Then they all stared at Alex. There was going to be trouble. Red heart trouble.

5

Seeing Red

"You're going to have the best decorated room for Valentine's Day," Alex told Mr. Parker when we got back from lunch. "We're going to decorate it for you!"

Alex, Ashley, Maria, and Barbara hurried to get bright red paper. Then they rushed back to their desks. In no time, they each had a small stack of hearts. Each heart had their name on it. Pretty soon everybody was cutting hearts. There were so many the piles overflowed and a few hearts fluttered to the floor.

"I've never seen this many hearts," Adam said.

I nodded. "Alex doesn't need so many valentines. She doesn't have that many friends."

"What are you going to do with all those hearts?" I asked Alex.

Alex was too busy cutting out valentines to think about it. "We'll make them," she said, "and you figure out what to do with them!"

Randy kept score to see who made the most valentines. Adam and I scooped up the bright red hearts and taped them to Mr. Parker's desk. We taped them to the chalkboard. We used lots of tape to make sure they wouldn't fall down.

Adam stopped by Alex's desk. "There are too many hearts. You have to stop."

Alex didn't look up at her brother. She was too busy cutting another heart. "I can't stop," she said. "I have to win the contest."

"But what are we supposed to do with all these hearts?" I asked her. I liked Valentine's Day. And decorating was fun. But Mr. Parker's room was so full of hearts I was beginning to see red.

Alex didn't have time to answer because just then Mr. Parker scribbled another sign and held it up. In bright green letters it said NO MORE RED HEARTS!

Nobody moved. Not even Alex.

Ashley looked at Barbara's hearts. Barbara looked at Maria's. Alex looked at them all. Then she looked at her own stack. Alex's pile was the smallest. If Alex didn't do something fast, she was going to lose the Red Heart Race!

6

The Red Heart Mess

"We have to make more valentines," Alex told Mr. Parker.

Mr. Parker leaned on his desk. Three red hearts stuck to his elbows. "You've made enough hearts."

"No, we haven't," Ashley blurted out.

I looked at the windows. They were covered with red hearts. I looked at the walls. There were hearts everywhere!

"Mr. Parker is right," Adam said. "There isn't a single spot left for another red heart."

"But we have to make more," Ashley said. Ashley hated to lose.

"No, we don't," Barbara said. She had the biggest valentine stack of them all. "I'm tired of making red hearts."

"Me, too," Maria said.

Most of the kids agreed there were enough hearts. Everybody, that is, except Alex and Ashley.

Mr. Parker plucked a valentine from his elbow. He got up to throw it in the trash. When he did, Ashley giggled. So did the rest of the class because there were red hearts stuck to his pants.

Mr. Parker tried to pull them off. I guess we used too much tape because the valentines stuck to his fingers. He tried to shake the hearts from his hands, but they were too sticky. The harder he shook his hands the more everybody giggled. Mr. Parker didn't look as if he thought it was funny. Instead, he looked very tired.

Mr. Parker shook and shook until the sticky red hearts finally fluttered off his fingers. Then they stuck on his shoes. His feet looked like giant red hearts. He had hearts on his pants, hearts on his elbows, and hearts on his feet. Our teacher was a red heart mess.

Mr. Parker grabbed a marker and scribbled. When he held up his new sign his letters looked big and serious.

VALENTINE'S DAY IS CANCELED!

Maria gasped and Barbara looked ready to cry. But Ashley turned around in her chair and glared at Alex. "This is all your fault," she said.

"Ashley's right," Adam said. "If Alex hadn't started this silly Red Heart Race, we could still have Valentine's Day."

I held my breath. I liked Ashley and I liked Adam, but when they ganged up on Alex there was bound to be trouble. Triplet trouble.

7

Ashley's Brilliant Idea

Adam and I didn't say a word as we walked home after school. Neither did Ashley or Alex. We walked until we were in front of the Oakridge Retirement Home.

I looked at my watch. It was exactly 3:14. We had one minute to wait. I looked at Ashley. Her lip stuck out in a big pout.

"I can't believe you ruined Valentine's Day for the whole class!" Ashley said to Alex.

Alex looked at the red hearts on her shoes and didn't say a word.

But Adam pointed his finger at Ashley. "It was your fault, too. You made just as many hearts as Alex."

"I made more," Ashley said proudly.

"Then it is your fault!" Alex told her sister.

Ashley stomped her foot. "Is not!"

I grabbed Ashley's and Alex's shoulders. It was exactly 3:15. "Stop shouting," I said. "There's Miss Crankshaw."

Miss Crankshaw waved out the window. Adam and I waved back. Ashley and Alex stopped fighting long enough to smile and wave, too.

"Miss Crankshaw probably doesn't get to have Valentine's Day either," Adam said. "She's not yelling about it."

Alex and Ashley both stared at Miss Crankshaw. I could tell they felt bad about fighting. "I wish we could do something to

make her Valentine's Day special," Alex said.

I nodded. "I bet she misses all her plants and things."

"I bet she misses visiting with us, too," Adam said.

Ashley looked at me. Then she looked at Adam and Alex. Ashley clapped her hands and shouted. "That's it!" she said. "That's the answer to our valentine mess!"

"What?" Alex asked.

Ashley smiled at Alex and said, "You're not the only one who can come up with brilliant ideas. Just wait until tomorrow!"

8

A Secret

Ashley wouldn't tell anyone her brilliant idea. The next morning she went straight to Mr. Parker and whispered something into his ear. Mr. Parker rubbed his chin and nodded.

Secrets aren't any fun if you feel left out. Ashley and Mr. Parker were leaving everyone out of their secret.

Mr. Parker cleared his throat. "We must gather up all of these Valentine's Day decorations. Barbara, will you be in charge?"

Barbara collected the valentine hearts in a brown paper bag. The only hearts that didn't go in the bag were the ones Alex had tied in her hair. Mr. Parker had really canceled Valentine's Day. He was even pulling the hearts off his desk and the windows.

That afternoon, Mr. Parker held up a new sign. It said FIELD TRIP TODAY!

I had a feeling that this field trip had something to do with Ashley's secret.

Mr. Parker led us down Filbert Street. Ashley walked right behind Mr. Parker.

Her giggling was starting to make me mad. I wasn't the only one.

"I don't like secrets," Adam mumbled.

"Me neither," Alex said.

Mr. Parker walked until he reached the Oakridge Retirement Home. Then he stopped. I looked at my watch. It was only 1:30. Miss Crankshaw wouldn't know to wave out her window. We were too early.

Suddenly, the door opened wide. There stood Miss Crankshaw wearing a big, friendly smile.

Mr. Parker was grinning, too. "Surprise!" he said. "Welcome to the Oakridge Retirement Home's Valentine's Day party!"

Miss Crankshaw waved us inside to meet all her friends. All the second-graders

decorated the Oakridge Retirement Home with our bag full of valentines. We put red hearts on the windows and the walls. We taped red hearts everywhere. Then we handed all of Miss Crankshaw's friends pretty red hearts that we had made. Alex gave Miss Crankshaw a red heart from her hair. That made everyone laugh.

Miss Crankshaw brought out a huge tray of her yummy cookies. They were heart-shaped, too. She gave Mr. Parker the biggest one. After we ate our cookies we played candy heart BINGO. Everybody laughed when Mr. Parker won all the candy hearts. He shared them with everyone.

I smiled at the Tucker triplets. Alex grinned big enough to show the space where her tooth used to be and Ashley giggled. Even Adam smiled. Mr. Parker hadn't canceled Valentine's Day after all. Thanks to the Tucker Triplets' Red Heart Race, it was the best Valentine's Day party ever!

Meet some new friends in a brand-new
series just right for <u>you</u>.
Starring **Baby-sitters Little Sister**
Karen Brewer...
and everyone else in the second grade.

Look for THE KIDS IN MS. COLMAN'S CLASS #1: TEACHERS PET.
Coming to your bookstore in September.

MC 195